This magical book belongs to:

_____

Disney's
Magical World
of Reading

1 101 Dalmatians

2 The Fox and the Hound

Adapted by Kathryn Knight
Art Direction by Andy Mangrum

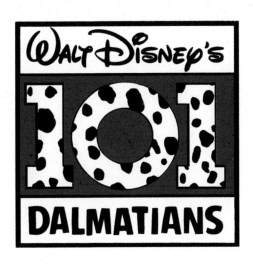

This is the story of two brave parents, ninety-nine puppies, and one of the greatest rescues of all time.

Roger Radcliff was a musician.
He lived in London with Pongo,
his pet Dalmatian dog.

One day, Roger got married.

His wife was named Anita.

She had a beautiful lady Dalmatian
named Perdita.

Pongo and Perdita fell in love, too.

Soon, Perdita and Pongo had
fifteen little puppies.
They were very proud and happy.
That very day, Anita's friend came.
She was not a nice friend.
She was Cruella De Vil!

"Where are the puppies?" she said.
"I just adore Dalmatian puppies!
I'll buy all of them!"
Roger said, "Oh, no, you won't.
They are *not* for sale."
"You fools!" Cruella cried.
"You'll be sorry!"
She stormed out of the house.

One night, Cruella sent Horace and
Jasper Badun to dognap the puppies!
The police looked
everywhere for the puppies.

Days and days went by.

The puppies were still not found.

"We have to find our puppies,"

Pongo said to Perdita.

"Tonight I will send the Twilight Bark.

I will let all the other dogs know

about our stolen puppies."

That night, Pongo sent the alarm:
"Bark, bark, bark, h-o-w-l!"
Pongo and Perdita waited.

Then a bark came back.
"It's the Great Dane!" said Pongo.
Pongo barked the message
about the missing puppies.

Danny the Great Dane told another dog,
"Fifteen Dalmatian puppies are stolen!
We have to send the message to all dogs!"
Danny's big deep bark sent the news
all over London.

Two other dogs
spread the news.
Then two more.

The Twilight Bark went everywhere.
An old sheepdog heard the news.
His name was the Colonel.
He lived on a farm with his friends—
a horse named the Captain
and a cat named Sergeant Tibs.

"Fifteen puppies stolen!" said the Colonel.
Tibs said, "Hmmm. I heard puppies barking
at the old De Vil house last night."
"But no one lives there now," said the Colonel.
"We must go and see what's going on."

The Colonel and Tibs went up to the house
and looked into a window.
They saw Horace and Jasper Badun.

And they saw puppies!
Not fifteen puppies.
Not even fifty puppies.
They counted *ninety-nine* puppies!

The Colonel went to send the Twilight Bark.
He sent the good news
that the puppies had been found.
Other dogs spread the news.
It went all the way to London.

Pongo and Perdita heard the news.
It did not take them long to go!
Off they went over the snow
to rescue their puppies!

Tibs was watching the house.
Cruella came to the house.
She was yelling at the men,
"I want their skins for fur coats!
I'll be back in the morning."
Then Cruella left.

Fur coats!

How awful!

Tibs could not believe it!

He had to save these poor puppies!

Tibs went through a broken window.

He said softly to one of the puppies,

"Tell everyone they must escape.

Cruella is after your coats!"

The Baduns were watching TV.

So Tibs led the puppies out of the room.

Quietly, quietly, quietly.

They had to find a hiding place.

But, oh, no!

The Baduns found them!

Jasper had them in a corner!

Tibs tried to protect the puppies!

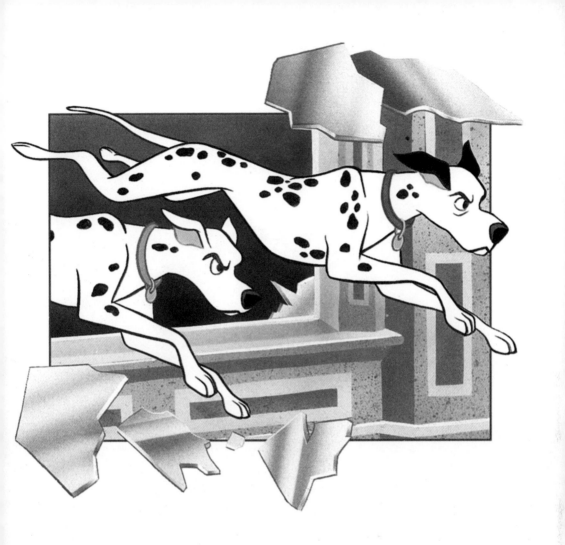

Meanwhile, the Colonel had met up
with Perdita and Pongo.
He led them to the De Vil house.
They arrived just in the nick of time.
They jumped through a window
to save their puppies!

Perdita went after Horace.

Pongo bit Jasper in the pants.

Tibs led the puppies out of the house.

He led them to the Captain's stable.

Perdita and Pongo dashed after the puppies.

"Are our fifteen all here?" asked Perdita.

The Captain said, "Your fifteen are here,
and there are more than that.

There are *ninety-nine!*"

"*Ninety-nine!*" said Pongo.

"Why did Cruella want *ninety-nine* puppies?"

There was silence for a moment.

Then one little puppy said,

"She was going to make fur coats out of us."

Perdita and Pongo were shocked.

"We'll take them *all* back with us," said Perdita.

"All ninety-nine!"

Perdita, Pongo and the puppies set off for home.

They rested in a blacksmith's shop.

But they left pawprints in the snow.

And Cruella spotted the pawprints!

She and the Baduns were after them!

Pongo had an idea.
He made the puppies
roll in some soot.
They all looked like black Labradors.
"Quick! Into this van!" said Pongo.
"It's going to London!"

As the van sped away,
Cruella spotted the dogs!
"Hmmm..." she said.
"I think I have been tricked.
After them!"

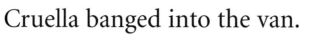

Cruella banged into the van.

But the van kept going.

Cruella and the Baduns crashed!

And the Dalmatians got away!

31

Back in London, Roger and Anita
hugged the tired puppies.
"Fourteen, fifteen," counted Roger,
"sixty-two—eighty—ninety-nine
puppies... plus Perdita and Pongo!
That's a hundred and one Dalmatians!"

Anita asked, "What are we going
to do with them all?"
"Why, we will keep them,
of course," said Roger.
"We'll buy a big house and have
a Dalmatian Plantation!"

And that's exactly what they did!

Walt Disney's
The Fox and the Hound

This is the story of two unlikely friends
who found out that caring and friendship
can last a lifetime.

One morning, Mrs. Tweed found a baby fox.

"I will name you Tod," she said.

"I will take care of you."

Down the road,

Amos had a puppy hound.

"I will name you Copper," he said.

"Chief and I will take care of you.

We will teach you to hunt."

Time went by.

Tod grew bigger every day.

Copper grew bigger, too.

One morning, Tod went out of

the farm and into the woods.

He ran into... guess who!

Copper!

"Oh, good! Someone to play with!"

thought Tod.

"He's a funny-looking dog,"

thought Copper.

Tod and Copper both said, "Hello."

Soon the fox and the hound

were very good friends.

Tod and Copper played all day!
They romped through the woods.
They chased each other.
They jumped into a pond together.
Splash!
They could not stop laughing.

Then it was time to go home.
"Let's play together every day,"
said Tod.
"Every day!" said Copper.
And they did.

But one morning, Copper was not there.

Tod looked for him at Amos's house.

He found his friend tied up.

He was very surprised.

Mrs. Tweed never tied *him* up.

Suddenly, Chief saw Tod.

"A fox!" growled Chief.

Chief leaped at Tod.

Tod was so afraid!

He ran right into the chickens!

Squawk! Growl! What a racket!

Tod ran all the way home.

Amos Slade was very mad.
He went to Mrs. Tweed's house.

"Keep your fox away from my hens!"
Amos growled. "Or else..."
Mrs. Tweed said, "Don't you dare
hurt my fox, Mr. Slade!
He's a good and kind pet.
He would not hurt your hens.
Now, go away!"

Mrs. Tweed knew that Tod
had not done anything wrong.
She kept him inside to keep him safe.

Tod missed his friend Copper.
Copper missed his friend Tod, too.
Then, one day, Copper saw Amos
and Chief with the car.
"Come, on, Copper," said Amos.
"I'm going to teach you to hunt!"

That same morning, Tod sneaked away.

"What a wonderful morning!" he sang.

"I can't wait to see Copper."

But what Tod saw made him sad.

Copper was leaving in a car.

And Tod did not know that Copper

would be gone a long, long time....

Days flew by.

Winter turned into Spring.

Tod had grown to be a big fox.

"How tall you are!" said his friends.

Rumble, rumble, rumble.

Amos's car drove by.

"Copper is back!" cried Tod with joy.

"I'll go see him tonight."

That night, Tod slipped out.

He ran over to Amos's house.

Copper was happy at first,

but then he said, "You have to go.

I am a hound now and I hunt foxes."

"But I'm not just any fox, Copper!

I'm your friend!" said Tod.

Suddenly, Chief woke up!

Then Amos woke up!

"After that fox!" yelled Amos.

Tod ran away as fast as he could.

Copper caught up with him.

"Run that way!" said the hound.

He pointed at a bridge.

"I'll lead them the other way.

I don't want them to find you."

But Chief *did* find Tod!

He ran after Tod up on the bridge!

All of a sudden, a train came.

Tod escaped, but Chief was not so lucky.

He tried to jump to the side.

But he fell off the bridge,

down into the stream below.

Tod felt very sad for Chief.
He slowly made his way home,
hoping that Chief would be all right.

Copper was sad, too... and mad!
He thought that Tod had hurt Chief.
"I'll hunt down that fox!" he said.

Mrs. Tweed knew it was time
to let Tod run free.
"Foxes should live in the woods,"
she said, as she took off his collar.
She took Tod to live in a safe place.
"Good-bye, Tod," she said kindly.

"What will I do now?" thought Tod.

He was so lonely.

But not for long.

Tod met a nice she-fox named Vixey,

and they fell in love.

Meanwhile, Amos was out hunting.
He and Copper were hunting for Tod!
But a huge bear came into their path.
With a great roar, the bear went after
Amos and Copper.
Tod heard the roaring and snarling.
He ran over, just as Copper
got hurt by the angry bear!

Tod raced to help his friend.
He did not care that Copper
had become a hunting dog.
Tod jumped on the bear and bit his ear.
He led the bear away to a bridge,
where the bear fell into the water below.
Tod had saved Copper and Amos!

But what was Amos doing?
Would Amos shoot him after all?
Copper jumped in front of his friend.
"If Amos shoots you, he will have to
shoot me, too," said Copper to his friend.

Amos put his gun down.

"Copper, you are right.

Thanks for saving us, little fox,"

said Amos. And he walked away.

Tod said, "Good-bye, Copper.

"I must run and go find Vixey."

"Good-bye, Tod, and thank you!"

called the hound after him.

Amos went to Mrs. Tweed's farm.
She was very surprised to see him.
"You were right, Mrs. Tweed,"
he told her. "Your fox is nice."
Mrs. Tweed smiled with pride.
She took care of Amos's hurt foot.
Amos and Mrs. Tweed became friends.

And Tod and Vixey were happy together.
"The two most beautiful things in
the world are love and friendship,"
Tod told Vixey.
Vixey agreed.

The End